W9-BYN-252

Too Big to Run

Look for all
the books in the

PET RESCUE CLUB
series

Too Big to Run

by Catherine Hapka
illustrated by Dana Regan

studio fun

A READER'S DIGEST COMPANY

White Plains, New York • Montréal, Québec • Bath, United Kingdom

cover illustration by Steve James
photo courtesy of Geoffrey Tischman

Published by Studio Fun International, Inc.
44 South Broadway, White Plains, NY 10601 U.S.A. and
Studio Fun International Limited,
The Ice House, 124-126 Walcot Street, Bath UK BA1 5BG
Illustration ©2015 Studio Fun International, Inc.
Text ©2015 ASPCA®
All rights reserved.
Studio Fun Books is a trademark of Studio Fun International, Inc.,
a subsidiary of The Reader's Digest Association, Inc.
Printed in China.
10 9 8 7 6 5 4 3 2 1
SL2/05/15

***The American Society for the Prevention of Cruelty to Animals (ASPCA®)
will receive a minimum guarantee from Studio Fun International, Inc. of $25,000
for the sale of ASPCA® products through December 2017.**

Comments? Questions? Call us at: 1-888-217-3346

Library of Congress Control Number: 2015939444

To all dogs, big and small

C.H.

1

Clinic Clients

"We're here, we're here!" Janey Simpson exclaimed breathlessly as she rushed into the Park View Critter Clinic. "It's Lolli's fault we're late."

Her friend Lolli Simpson giggled and followed Janey into the vet clinic's cozy waiting room. "She's right, it's my fault. I had to feed the goats and sheep before we came."

Lolli's family lived on a small farm. They had two pet goats and a sheep. One of Lolli's chores was to feed the animals on weekends.

"That's okay," Zach Goldman said. "Mom's not finished yet anyway."

"Yeah, she has one more patient to see," Adam Santos said.

Zach's mother was a veterinarian who owned the Critter Clinic. She had agreed to drive Zach, Janey, Lolli, and Adam to the animal shelter after she finished with her morning clients.

It was easy to guess who her last patient was, since there was only one animal in the waiting room—a cute little Chihuahua. He was wagging his tail while Adam petted him.

"This is Pepper," Zach told Janey and Lolli. The little dog barked when Zach said his name.

"Aw, he's adorable!" Janey perched on the edge of one of the waiting room chairs and rubbed Pepper's head. He licked her hand with his tiny pink tongue and wagged his tail even harder.

The Chihuahua's owner smiled. She was a tall woman a little older than Janey's mom. "Thanks," she said. "He loves everyone. That's why he makes such a good therapy dog."

"Therapy dog?" Janey echoed, a little confused. Pepper was smaller than most of her stuffed animals! How could he be a therapy dog? "Do you mean Pepper leads blind people around?"

"No, that's a service dog," Adam said. "Therapy dogs are different. Mrs. Reed was just telling us all about it. She and Pepper visit hospitals and nursing homes every week. It makes people feel better when they can interact with a friendly animal."

Adam sounded interested in what he was telling the girls. That was no surprise, since Adam was interested in everything having to do with dogs. He ran a successful dog-sitting business even though he was only nine.

"That makes sense," Janey said. "Being with animals always makes me feel better." She sighed. "Even if it doesn't happen often enough."

"Janey is crazy about animals," Lolli told Mrs. Reed. "But she can't have any pets because her dad is allergic to anything with fur or feathers."

"Oh, dear." Mrs. Reed looked sympathetic. "Well, at least you have the Pet Rescue Club, right?"

Janey's eyes widened. "You know about the Pet Rescue Club?" she exclaimed. "We're famous!"

Zach laughed. "Not exactly," he said. "Adam and I were just telling her about it."

Janey, Lolli, Adam, and Zach had started the Pet Rescue Club to help animals in need in their town. So far they'd helped find great new homes for several animals, including a dog, a cat, and even a pony.

Janey had been good friends with Lolli and Adam even before starting the Pet Rescue Club. At first she hadn't been sure Zach would make a good member. She still thought he joked around too much. But he was a computer expert and helped run the group's blog. Besides, he knew a lot about animals because of his mother's job.

"It sounds like you kids have done a lot of good for homeless animals so far," Mrs. Reed said. "Let me know if Pepper and I can ever be of any help."

"Thanks," Lolli said. "How did Pepper become a therapy dog, anyway? Did he have to take special classes? Because I bet my dog would love to visit people—he's super friendly."

Janey gasped. "Oh, you're right!" she exclaimed. "Roscoe would be a perfect therapy dog!"

Zach laughed. "Yeah, except it might be a problem if he tries to sit in people's laps like Pepper does."

"True. He's a little bigger than Pepper." Lolli grinned at Mrs. Reed. "He's part Lab, part Rottweiler, and part who knows what."

"Therapy dogs come in all shapes and sizes," Mrs. Reed replied with a smile. "The only important things are the right kind of temperament and some basic training."

"Really?" Zach looked surprised.

The woman nodded, bending down to pat Pepper. "Actually, I've been thinking about getting a second dog myself, and I was thinking I might look for a larger one this time," she said. "Pepper is perfect for snuggling with elderly folks. But children can be a little too rambunctious for such a small, delicate dog. A medium-sized critter might be better for visiting them."

"I know the perfect place for you to find

a dog," Janey exclaimed. "The Third Street Animal Shelter! They have all sizes!"

The other members of the Pet Rescue Club nodded. They all volunteered at the shelter, which had helped them place their very first rescue animal.

"Yes, I was thinking of looking there," Mrs. Reed said.

"We're going there after Mom sees Pepper," Zach told her excitedly. "You could come with us!"

The woman chuckled. "Thanks, Zach. But Pepper and I are scheduled to visit a nursing home this afternoon." She shrugged. "Actually, Pepper and I are pretty busy for the next few weeks. But maybe we'll stop by the shelter next month. I'm sure we'll be able to find our new therapy-dog friend there."

Janey frowned slightly. Next month? That seemed like forever away!

"Are you sure you don't have time to go to the shelter sooner?" she asked. "It's open every day of the week. Even tomorrow—Sunday!"

Lolli poked her. "Don't be impatient, Janey," she said gently. "Mrs. Reed will go when she's ready."

Janey knew her friend was right. Lolli was always thoughtful and tried to see things from other people's point of view.

But Janey liked to look at things from animals' points of view. "Okay," she said. "The thing is, I just know there are plenty of medium-sized dogs in the shelter that would love a new home pronto!"

"Pronto?" Zach said.

"That's Janey's new word," Lolli told him. "It means immediately."

"Oh." Zach rolled his eyes, then looked at Mrs. Reed. "Janey likes to pick out weird new words and use them a lot."

"Pronto, eh?" Mrs. Reed winked at Janey. "Well, we'll see. Maybe we can find a time

to get over there sooner after all—I mean, pronto."

Janey smiled. "I hope so."

Just then the vet assistant poked his head out of one of the doors. "Mrs. Reed?" he said. "The doctor is almost finished with her last patient. Why don't you and Pepper come into exam room two and get settled. She'll be with you soon."

"Thanks, Russ." The woman stood up and whistled. "Come on, Pepper. Time for your booster shots!"

Pepper looked up, alert. Then he barked and trotted at his owner's heel as she followed the tech into the room.

Janey sighed as she watched them go. "I wish I had a Chihuahua like Pepper," she said. "He's so cute!"

"You wish you could take home every dog you meet," Lolli reminded her with a smile.

"Yeah," Zach said. "Wait until you see the dog in exam room one! You'll definitely want him!"

"Really?" Janey glanced at the closed door to exam room one. "What kind of dog is he?"

Zach and Adam traded a grin. "You'll see," Adam said.

2

Too Big to Run?

Janey wanted to ask more questions. But before she could, the door to exam room one opened. Out walked the biggest dog Janey had ever seen! The dog had floppy ears, droopy jowls, and a sweet expression.

"What in the world is that?" Janey cried loudly.

Lolli giggled. "Is it a dog, or a bear?"

The dog's owner walked out, too. He was a lean young man dressed in shorts and a sweatshirt. He smiled at the kids.

"This is Maxi," he said. "She's big, but she's friendly—it's okay to pet her if you like."

"Maxi is a mastiff," Adam told the others.

"Oh, right," Janey said. "I recognize her now from my books. I read that mastiffs are a giant breed—and now I see that it's true!"

Janey loved to read books about animals. She was interested in all kinds of dogs and cats. She'd seen pictures of mastiffs before.

But she'd never seen one in person. Maxi looked even bigger than Janey expected.

The dog drooled happily and wagged her tail as the kids walked toward her. But when she took a step, she limped a little.

"What's wrong?" Lolli asked. "Is she injured?"

The young man sighed. "Yes, that's why we're here. She's my jogging buddy, and we were on a run yesterday when she started limping. Dr. Goldman says poor Maxi blew out both her knees."

"Ouch." Janey scratched the mastiff's massive head. "That sounds painful."

Just then Zach's mother bustled out from the back room. "Here you go, Matthew," she said, handing the young man a bottle. "I found enough pills to last Maxi through the weekend. If you stop by on Monday afternoon, I'll have the rest for you by then."

"Thanks, Dr. G," Matthew said. "I hope these will make poor Maxi feel better."

"They'll help." Dr. Goldman patted the big dog. "But as I mentioned, I'm afraid the only thing that will really help her long-term is surgery."

Matthew winced. "I know, I know," he said. "I just don't know if I can afford it—at least not anytime soon."

"What do you mean?" Janey asked.

"I just graduated from college," Matthew said with a sigh. "I'm working two jobs to make ends meet as it is. I don't know how I'm going to scrape together enough money for Maxi's surgery!"

"Well, we can try the meds for now and

let her get plenty of rest," Dr. Goldman said. "That should make her feel a little better."

"Thanks, doc." Matthew stuck the pill bottle in the pocket of his shorts. Then he snapped a leash onto Maxi's collar. "Come on, big girl," he said. "We'd better head for home."

"Walking only, remember?" The vet said with a smile. "No jogging."

"Promise," Matthew said. "See you on Monday, doc!"

The kids gave Maxi a few more pats, and then she and her owner left. Dr. Goldman looked worried as she watched them go.

"Why did you tell him not to jog home?" Janey asked the vet.

"Because Matthew is a serious runner," Dr. Goldman answered. "Unfortunately, mastiffs don't make very good jogging companions. They're too big and heavy to handle that much extra stress on their joints."

Janey was surprised. "Maxi is too big to run?" she said. "I thought all dogs loved running around."

"A gentle lope around the park is one thing," Dr. Goldman said. "But miles every day on pavement is another matter."

Just then Russ stuck his head out into the waiting room. "Pepper is next, doctor," he said.

"Coming," the vet replied. She glanced at the kids. "Pepper is my last patient of the morning. As soon as we're finished, I can drive you over to the shelter."

"We'll be here, Mom," Zach said.

"Thanks," Lolli added.

The vet smiled and disappeared into exam room two. Zach flopped into one of the waiting room chairs.

"We should have a Pet Rescue Club meeting while we wait," he suggested. "We haven't met any needy pets since we found Lola the pony a new home."

"True," Adam said. "Maybe we should post on the blog asking for our readers to suggest other animals that need help."

"Good idea," Lolli agreed. "Janey, what do you think?"

"Huh?" Janey hadn't really been listening. She was still thinking about Maxi and her sore knees.

Lolli poked her in the arm. "We said, should we post on the blog to find more animals to help?"

"Haven't you guys been paying attention?" Janey said. "We already know an animal who needs our help. Two of them, actually."

"We do?" Lolli's big brown eyes got even bigger with surprise. "Who?"

"I know," Adam spoke up. "Mrs. Reed's new dog, right?"

"Yes, that's one of the animals I was thinking of," Janey said. "Maybe if we figure out which medium-sized dog at the shelter would make the best therapy dog, she'll adopt it pronto."

Zach nodded. "Okay. Who's the second animal?"

"Maxi," Janey replied. "Didn't you hear what Matthew said? He can't afford to pay for her surgery. Maybe we can help."

"How?" Zach scratched his head. "I just spent all of my allowance on some cool new stickers for my skateboard."

But Lolli was nodding. "I think I know what you're thinking," she said. "We could have a fundraiser!"

"Raise money for Maxi's surgery?" Adam nodded thoughtfully. "That's a good idea."

Janey grinned. "I know. So let's start thinking!"

3

Big Ideas

Janey was still thinking about Maxi as the kids all piled into Dr. Goldman's car a little while later. "You said surgery will fix Maxi's knees, right?" she asked as the vet started the engine. "Then she'll be as good as new?"

"Well, she should be much more comfortable, yes," the vet said. "But if Matthew keeps asking her to run with him, it won't be long until she's right back where she started."

"You mean she'll probably hurt her knees again?" Adam sounded worried.

Dr. Goldman shrugged. "As I said, mastiffs aren't built for lots of running."

Janey traded a look with her friends. "We should still try to raise money for the surgery," she said.

"Definitely," Lolli agreed. "Matthew will probably stop taking Maxi jogging if he understands it's hurting her."

Dr. Goldman looked at the kids in the rearview mirror. "Raise money for surgery?" she said. "Is this a new Pet Rescue Club project?"

"Yes," Janey said. With her friends' help, she told the vet about their idea.

By the time they finished, Dr. Goldman was nodding. "I think that's a super plan," she said. "I'll be happy to donate my time free of charge. So you'll just need to raise enough to cover the cost of the surgical supplies and medications."

"Hooray!" Lolli cheered. "Thanks, Dr. Goldman!"

The vet smiled. "You're welcome. So what kind of fundraiser are you planning?"

"We're not sure yet," Janey said. Pepper's appointment hadn't taken very long, so the kids hadn't had much time to talk about ideas. "But I'm sure we can come up with something pronto."

"I hope you have an extra-large operating table, Mom," Zach said with a laugh.

"Yeah." Lolli nodded. "I thought Roscoe was pretty big until I saw Maxi!"

Adam grinned. "She's almost as big as Lola the pony!"

Dr. Goldman chuckled. "Believe it or not, Maxi isn't the largest mastiff I've ever seen.

The females are usually a little bit smaller than the males."

....

They arrived at the shelter. "Call me when you're ready to leave," said Dr. Goldman. "I'll be at the clinic taking care of some paperwork, so I can pick you up whenever you like."

When the kids entered, there were several people in the lobby. Kitty, a worker at the shelter, was handing a piece of paper to an older couple. The husband was holding a crate. A cute dog with a pointy nose was

peering out through the mesh door.

"Oh, did Peanut get adopted?" Janey exclaimed, rushing over to peer in at the dog. "That's great! He's an awesome dog."

When Peanut, a dachshund mix with short legs and silky fur, had first arrived at the shelter a couple of weeks earlier, he'd been pretty shy. So Janey spent time with him to help socialize him to new people and situations. He got comfortable and relaxed pretty quickly and then became very friend- ly and playful.

"We know." The wife smiled at all the kids. "He's a sweetheart."

"Congratulations on the new addition to your family," Kitty said. "Just call us if you have any questions or problems, okay?"

"Thank you." The husband leaned down

to look at the dog. "Come on, Peanut. Let's go home."

The couple hurried out. Kitty was still smiling.

"I think Peanut is a perfect match for those two," she said. "They both work from home, so he'll get lots of attention."

"That's great," Adam said. "Peanut is a great dog, but he needed just the right home."

"Yeah." Lolli giggled. "Peanut definitely wouldn't want to live with Matthew, for instance. No way could he keep up with all that jogging on those short little legs!"

"Matthew is a dog owner we just met at the vet clinic," Zach told Kitty. "He's a serious jogger, and he has this huge mastiff named Maxi who runs with him."

"Really?" Kitty looked surprised. "I didn't think mastiffs made good running companions."

"That's exactly what my mom said," Zach told her. "She says all that running wrecked Maxi's knees."

The other kids joined in to tell Kitty all about Maxi and Matthew and their idea to have a fundraiser for them.

"Wow," Kitty said when they finished. "What a great idea! Why don't you guys brainstorm while you clean some kennels?"

Adam laughed. "Is that your way of telling us to clean some kennels?"

Kitty laughed, too. "Yes, it is. Now get to work, kids!"

"Pronto!" Janey added, which made everyone laugh again.

Soon the four members of the Pet Rescue Club were hard at work cleaning kennels in the shelter's dog room. It wasn't Janey's favorite job at the shelter, but she didn't mind it too much, because she knew it helped the animals that lived there.

Besides, working in the kennel room gave her a chance to check out the dogs there. "Mrs. Reed wants a medium-sized dog," she reminded Lolli, who was working beside her. "That gives us plenty of choices. There are lots of medium-sized dogs here."

Lolli nodded. "How about Daisy the corgi? She's pretty friendly."

"Maybe," Janey agreed. "Or there's that terrier mix, or maybe…"

She cut herself off as the door opened and Kitty hurried in. "Did you guys finish cleaning out Peanut's kennel?" the shelter worker called. "Because we already have a new resident for it."

"Really?" Janey stepped into the aisle and saw that Kitty was leading a wiggly black dog with perky ears and a long snout.

"Doesn't he have to go in the quarantine room first?" Adam asked.

"The quarantine room is full right now," Kitty replied. "Besides, this dog's former owners brought his vet records. He's up to date on everything." She sighed. "They can't keep him because they're moving."

Janey traded a sad look with her friends. She couldn't believe so many people gave up their pets when they moved, or for other reasons that didn't seem very important to Janey.

The dog sniffed at Zach, his tail wagging nonstop. Then he barked and leaped against his legs, as if trying to climb right up into Zach's arms.

Zach laughed and hoisted him up for a hug. "Aw, he's really friendly!" he exclaimed as the dog eagerly licked his face from chin to forehead. "What's his name?"

"Ace," Kitty said. "He's a Lab mix."

"He's small for a lab mix," Adam commented.

"Yes," Janey said with a thoughtful smile. "I'd definitely call him medium-sized, wouldn't you?"

"I suppose so." Kitty took Ace back from Zach and led him to the empty kennel. "Here you go, boy. I hope you like your new home."

"Don't worry," Janey said, still smiling. "I doubt he'll be there for long."

"Hope not." Kitty headed for the door. "Well, I'd better go finish his paperwork."

She hurried out. Zach kneeled and poked his fingers in through the bars so Ace could lick them. Meanwhile, Lolli stared at Janey.

"Let me guess," she said. "You think Ace should be Mrs. Reed's new therapy dog?"

"He's perfect!" Janey stuck her fingers

in beside Zach's and giggled as Ace licked them, then leaped away to sniff at his new water dish. "He's definitely friendly, right? And he's medium-sized."

Adam looked dubious as he watched Ace race over to stare at the dog in the next kennel. "He seems pretty hyper," he said. "I'm not sure that's going to work for a therapy dog."

Janey shrugged. "He's just excited to meet us. I'm sure he'll be fine once he has a new owner and a new job as a therapy dog to keep him busy." She straightened up and looked at her friends. "Okay, that's one animal helped!" she declared. "Now let's talk about Maxi's fundraiser."

4

Brainstorming

By Monday at lunchtime, the Pet Rescue Club still hadn't settled on what kind of fundraiser to have for Maxi. They'd been too busy to talk much at the shelter on Saturday. On Sunday, Janey had plans with her family and Adam had several extra dog-sitting clients. So the kids hadn't been able to meet then.

"How about a bake sale?" Janey licked some crumbs off her fingers. "My mom's gardening club had one last year. It was fun."

"A bake sale?" Zach wrinkled his nose. "Sounds kind of girly."

"What's wrong with being girly?" Janey shot back.

"It could be a bake sale where we just sold dog treats, maybe," Adam suggested.

"Do you know how to make dog treats?" Lolli asked.

Adam shrugged. "No. But we could look up recipes on the Internet."

"Sounds complicated," Zach said. "Anyway, buying all those ingredients would be expensive. We'd have to sell a whole lot of dog treats to make enough to pay for Maxi's surgery."

"Maybe he's right." Lolli sipped her drink "We need something simpler."

"And something that will make a lot of money," Janey added.

Adam shrugged. "Okay. What about an auction? We could ask businesses to donate stuff and then auction it off."

"That sounds pretty complicated, too," Zach said.

Janey nodded. "And it would take too long," she said. "Maxi needs help pronto, remember?"

By the time the bell rang to end lunch,

nobody had come up with a good plan. Janey felt frustrated.

"We need to think of something," she said. "Let's meet after school."

"I can't," Adam said. "I'm going to the dentist."

"And I told my mom I'd help update the computers at the clinic right after school," Zach said.

Janey frowned. How were they going to help Maxi if they couldn't even find a time to meet, let alone come up with a good idea for a fundraiser? "Okay, what about tomorrow after school?" she said.

"That's fine with me," Lolli agreed.

Adam shrugged. "I only have a couple of clients," he said. "I could meet you guys right after that."

"I'm in," Zach said. "But wait—shouldn't we tell Matthew about all this?"

"Definitely," Lolli agreed as she gathered up her lunch bag. "Maybe he'll have some fundraising ideas."

"Matthew's supposed to stop by and pick up more medicine today, remember?" Zach said. "Maybe I'll see him while I'm at the clinic."

"If you do, tell him about our plan," Janey said. "In the meantime, everyone keep thinking."

. . . .

After school, Janey and Lolli walked to the animal shelter. Lolli's father had agreed to pick them up there later.

"Is Ace still here?" Janey asked Kitty when they walked in.

Kitty nodded. "Yes, he's here," she said. "I haven't even had time to put his picture on the website yet."

"We could take his picture if you want," Lolli offered.

"Thanks, that would be great." Kitty reached under the desk for a digital camera. "You could take him for a walk in the courtyard and try to get some pictures there." She laughed. "Good luck getting him to stay still long enough to get a good shot!"

Janey grabbed a leash off the rack near the dog room door. Volunteers at the shelter weren't allowed to take animals off the property without a staff person along. But they could take dogs into the enclosed courtyard at the back of the building.

"Hi there, Acey-Wacey!" Janey sang

out as she and Lolli reached the new dog's kennel. "Ready for your close-up? We're going to make you look adorable!"

"I'm surprised you're so excited about taking his picture," Lolli said. "What if someone sees him on the website and adopts him before Mrs. Reed gets to meet him?"

"Don't worry, I already thought of that." Janey opened the kennel door and smiled as Ace rushed out and leaped against her legs. "I'm going to e-mail the pictures we take to Zach's mom and ask her to forward them to Mrs. Reed."

"Oh!" Lolli's eyes widened. "Good idea."

Ace pulled eagerly on the leash as they headed out of the dog room. "Hang on, Ace," Janey said with a giggle. "Wait for us!"

Ace barked and spun around, getting the

leash tangled around his legs. Janey untangled it, then hurried toward the door.

The courtyard was small but sunny. It was paved around the outside, but the middle part was grass. The shelter building's walls surrounded it on three sides, with a high brick wall at the back.

Ace barked as he dashed onto the grass. After that, he hardly stopped moving. He

leaped up to snap at a passing butterfly, dug at the ground, and sniffed at everything.

"Wow," Lolli said. "He sure has a lot of energy."

"He'll need it to be a therapy dog," Janey said. "It sounds like Mrs. Reed goes to a lot of places. Now hand me the camera and let's get started on our photo shoot!"

....

"There, that's done." Janey looked up from her tablet computer. "Now let's brainstorm ideas for Maxi."

She was in Lolli's sunny purple-painted bedroom. The two of them had just sent an e-mail to Dr. Goldman telling her about Ace. They'd attached the best pictures from their photo session. A lot of the pictures hadn't turned out very well, since Ace didn't like to stand still. But they'd found a few good ones.

"Okay." Lolli leaned back against her pillows. "We already decided not to do a bake sale. Or a car wash. Or a silent auction." She ticked off each thing on her fingers.

"Right." Janey closed her e-mail program. "Maybe we should look for ideas online."

"Yeah." Lolli sat up and leaned closer. "There are probably lots of sites about that."

Janey nodded and typed "raising money to help animals" into a search engine. She scanned the first few items that came up, but nothing sounded too promising.

Then she spotted something farther down the list. "Look at this," she said with a giggle. "It's a site of pictures of cats dressed up like bankers and stuff."

"Ooh, cute!" Lolli grinned. "Let's look."

"Okay—but only for a second. Then we have to get back to work." Janey clicked on the link.

Forty minutes later, the two girls were giggling over a photo of a cat wearing a ballerina's tutu. Lolli's mother poked her head into the room.

"Janey, your mom's here to pick you up," she said.

Janey gulped. "Oops," she said to Lolli. "I guess we got a little distracted."

"That's okay," Lolli said, though she looked worried, too. "Maybe Adam or Zach has thought of something good."

5

Meeting and Greeting

"Thanks, sweetie." Dr. Goldman leaned over Zach's shoulder and peered at the computer screen. "You've been a lot of help today."

Zach shrugged, spinning around in the reception chair and glancing around the clinic waiting room. "You're welcome. It's kind of fun working here. You know, sometimes."

He was surprised to realize that was true. Up until recently, he'd hated having to spend time at the vet clinic. It smelled like disinfectant, and he wasn't allowed to ride his skateboard in the waiting room even though the tile floor was perfect for it.

But ever since joining the Pet Rescue Club, it hadn't seemed so boring. It was fun to help out with the animals. Besides, his mom paid him extra allowance to keep her computer system up to date. Zach was better than anyone else in the family at computer stuff. Even his older brothers admitted it. And his dad worked at home and was hopeless when it came to technology. He needed Zach's help a lot.

Zach's mother clicked a few keys. "Oh, look, there's an e-mail from Janey," she said.

She opened it. Several photos were attached to the message.

Zach scanned the text. "Oh, right, that's the new dog at the shelter," he told his mom. "Janey thinks he'd be the perfect new therapy dog for Mrs. Reed."

"Yes, I saw that dog this morning," his mother said. "He cut his paw on something and Kitty asked me to take a look."

"He's great, isn't he?" Zach smiled as he remembered how Ace had slurped his face. "I bet Mrs. Reed and Pepper will love him!"

"Maybe." His mother didn't sound too sure. "He seemed a bit, er, lively. But it can't hurt to forward the pictures to her and see what she says."

Zach stretched and stood up. "Do you need me to do anything else?" he asked. Two Siamese cats were waiting for his mother in one of the exam rooms, and the waiting room was empty.

But it didn't stay that way for long.
The door opened, and a woman came in
carrying a two-year-old girl in one arm and
a large gray tabby cat in the other.

"Hello, Ms. Patel," Zach's mother greeted
her. "This is my son Zach. Zach, this is Ms.
Patel and her daughter Olivia."

"Hi," Zach said.

"Hello, Zach, it's nice to meet you," the

woman said. The toddler just stared at Zach and sucked on her fingers.

Zach glanced at the cat. "Your cat looks sort of like ours, except ours is orange instead of gray. His name's Mulberry."

"This is Toby. He hates being in a crate." Ms. Patel set the cat down. He stretched, then wandered over and meowed at Zach.

Zach laughed and bent down to tickle the cat's chin. "He's talkative."

His mother checked her watch. "You're a little early," she told Ms. Patel. "I'll be with you in a few minutes, all right?"

"No hurry." Ms. Patel spread a small blanket on the floor and set Olivia on it. She dumped a bag of toys beside the toddler, then sat back and sighed. "It feels good to relax!"

Dr. Goldman chuckled, then glanced at the counter. A large pill bottle was sitting there. "Matthew hasn't picked up his meds yet?"

Zach shook his head. He'd been watching for Maxi's owner. "I hope he gets here soon. I want to tell him we're going to help Maxi get her surgery."

His mother nodded, then disappeared into the exam room. Zach sat on one of the chairs. Toby jumped up beside him and started purring.

"He's really friendly," Zach said, petting the cat and watching Olivia play with some plastic blocks. "Hey, I wonder if cats can be therapy animals, too? Maybe Mulberry could do it."

"Therapy animals?" Ms. Patel echoed.

"Yeah." Zach smiled as Toby head-butted him. "I know this lady who takes her dog to nursing homes and stuff to visit people."

"Oh, yes, I've heard about that." Ms. Patel nodded. "My husband's father is in a nursing home, and he loves when animals come to visit."

Before Zach could respond, the clinic's front door opened. Maxi walked in, followed by Matthew. Olivia's eyes widened.

"Doggy!" she shrieked loudly.

Maxi pricked her ears. "Oh, dear," Ms. Patel said, bending to pick up her daughter. "What a large dog! Watch out, Toby."

"It's okay," Matthew said. "Maxi loves kids and cats. She's great with my nieces. And she plays with my neighbor's cat, Ralphie. Maxi's big, but very gentle."

Zach stepped over and gave Maxi a head rub. "Hi again, Maxi. How are your knees feeling?"

Matthew smiled, but he looked worried. "The medicine makes her feel better, but she's still limping a little." He sighed. "That's why I'm so late getting here. I just got off work, and since Maxi can't run with me right now, I figured I'd walk her here so we get to spend a little time together."

"Is she really gentle?" Ms. Patel asked. "I think Olivia would like to say hi."

Zach glanced at the toddler. She was wiggling in her mother's arms, reaching out toward the big dog.

"She's fine." Matthew smiled. "Come here, big girl. Sit."

Maxi sat at Matthew's feet, her tongue lolling out as Ms. Patel stepped toward her and put Olivia down. The little girl cooed and grabbed at the big dog, patting her on the head with both hands.

"Gently, Olivia," Ms. Patel said. "Just like when you pet Toby."

Olivia giggled and tugged on the dog's

ear. Maxi looked surprised, but didn't move. Matthew laughed.

"Good girl," he said, rubbing her head. "See? I told you—she loves kids."

Zach grinned. "I think someone else wants to meet her." He pointed at Toby, who was sniffing cautiously at Maxi's tail. When the dog wagged it, the cat leaped back and hissed.

"Oh, Tobes." Ms. Patel chuckled. "He's not used to dogs."

Suddenly Zach remembered the medication. He grabbed the bottle. "Here," he said, handing it to Matthew. "Mom said to give you these."

"Thanks." Matthew pocketed the bottle of pills. "I hope they help."

"Yeah. But surgery will help more, right?" Zach said. "My friends and I had an idea about that. We want to have a fundraiser to pay for it!"

"What?" Matthew looked startled. "What do you mean?"

Zach told him about the Pet Rescue Club. "So this is our new project," he finished with a grin. "Helping Maxi!"

"Wow!" Matthew grinned back. "That's amazing! Are you sure you guys want to do this?"

"I think it sounds like a wonderful idea," Ms. Patel put in. She was stroking Maxi's head while Olivia patted the big dog's side. Maxi was sitting quietly, her tongue lolling out of her mouth. Zach was pretty sure she was enjoying the attention.

"Okay." Matthew scratched his head, still looking stunned. "I mean, I wish I could pay for it myself. But if this is the fastest way to get Maxi feeling better…"

"It is," Zach assured him. "We aren't sure what fundraiser we're doing yet, though, so let us know if you think of any good ideas."

"Will do." Matthew looked happy as he leaned down and gave Maxi a big hug. "Did you hear that, girl? You'll be as good as new soon!"

"Yeah," Zach said. "That doesn't mean she can start jogging again, though. Mom says it's not good for such a big dog to put stress on her joints like that."

"Really?" Now Matthew looked less

happy. "But I work so much that our daily runs are really the only quality time we get to spend together. I'm not sure how I'll fit everything in if she has to stay home."

"Oh." Zach wasn't sure what to say to that. "Um…"

Just then Russ called Ms. Patel in to the exam room. At the same time, Matthew's cell phone rang. He answered, then waved good-bye to Zach as he headed out with Maxi following.

Zach stared after him, a little worried by what Matthew had just said.

Then he shrugged. They could figure that stuff out later. First they had to come up with a fundraising idea.

6

A Walk in the Park

"Hi guys," Kitty said with a smile as Janey, Lolli, and Zach walked into the shelter the next afternoon. "Where's Adam?"

"He had to take care of some clients right after school," Lolli said. "He's meeting us here in a little while."

Janey nodded, feeling impatient. The group still hadn't come up with a good idea for their fundraiser.

"I hope Adam gets here soon," she said. "We need the whole Pet Rescue Club to come up with the perfect idea."

"In the meantime, why don't you help me walk some dogs?" Kitty suggested. "I was going to take Patch to the park. If you guys come along, we could take a second dog with him."

That made Janey forget about her problems, at least for a moment. "How about Ace?" she said eagerly. "I bet he'd like some exercise."

Kitty chuckled. "I know he would. But he's not quite ready to walk in public yet," she said. "We're still working on his leash manners. Besides, one of the other workers took him out for some exercise earlier. Apparently, he tossed a ball for Ace for almost an hour and Ace never got tired."

Zach laughed. "Yeah, that sounds like Ace." He glanced at Janey. "That reminds me. My mom got those pictures you guys sent her yesterday."

"Great!" Janey said. "Did she forward them to Mrs. Reed?"

"I think so." Zach shrugged. "Mom wasn't sure Ace would be a good therapy dog, though. He's too hyper."

Janey frowned. "He's not that hyper. Anyway, I'm sure Mrs. Reed can handle him."

"Do you know someone who might want to adopt Ace?" Kitty asked. "That would be great. He's not a dog who would work for just anyone. He'll definitely need a special home."

"Mrs. Reed is definitely special," Janey

said. "I sent some pictures to her. I'm sure she'll love Ace."

"Great." Kitty checked her watch, sounding distracted. "Come on, we'd better get moving."

A few minutes later the four of them left the shelter. Kitty was holding a leash attached to Patch, a scruffy looking terrier

cross. Janey was walking an apricot-colored miniature poodle named Peaches.

"Follow me," Kitty said, setting off along the sidewalk. "What a nice day!"

Janey nodded. It was warm and sunny. Lots of people were out enjoying the pleasant weather.

"Look, Mommy!" a little boy cried from across the street. "Doggies!"

The boy and his mother looked both ways, then hurried across. "Excuse me," the woman said. "My son loves animals. Can he pet your dogs?"

"Yes, and thanks for asking first," Kitty replied with a smile. "Not every dog is friendly, but these two definitely are. Go ahead, young man."

Mother and son cooed over the dogs for a few minutes. After they moved on, an elderly man stopped to admire Patch, telling a long story about how he had a dog just like him as a child.

By the time the man said good-bye, Janey felt a little impatient. Were they ever going to make it to the park?

Finally they arrived. There were even more people there enjoying the nice day. And most of them seemed eager to come over and pat the dogs. Patch and Peaches both seemed to like the attention.

Not Janey, though. She wished everyone would leave them alone. Maybe then they'd be able to talk about their fundraising ideas.

She sighed as a young woman came over

leading a little girl who looked about four. "Hello," the young woman said. "This is Saffron, and I'm Rachel."

"She's my nanny," Saffron informed Janey and the others. "My mommy and daddy both have very important jobs."

"That's nice," Kitty said with a smile. "Would you like to pet the doggies?"

"Thanks." The nanny smiled back. "She's crazy about animals."

"Good doggie!" Saffron said loudly, lunging toward Patch.

The dog backed off a few steps, looking worried. "Carefully, Saffie," Rachel said. "Don't scare him."

"Boo!" the little girl yelled, grabbing for Patch again.

This time the terrier cross dashed behind
Kitty to get away. Janey rolled her eyes. Little
Saffron might be crazy about animals, but
she wasn't very good at petting them!

Meanwhile Saffron grabbed for Peaches.
The tiny poodle stood her ground, wagging
her tail uncertainly.

"Nice doggie!" Saffron cried, smacking
Peaches on the head.

"Oh, dear," the nanny said, yanking the

little girl away. "I'm so sorry!"

"Good girl, Peaches," Kitty said, picking up the poodle and cuddling her. Once the nanny had dragged her charge away, apologizing all the while, Kitty glanced at Janey and the others. "Wow, Peaches really handled that well. Maybe she should be your friend's new therapy dog."

"No," Janey said. "Peaches is too small. Mrs. Reed wants a medium-sized dog. Like Ace."

"Oh, okay, too bad." Kitty gave Peaches a kiss on the head and set her down. "Anyway, Peaches shouldn't be too difficult to adopt out. Small dogs are usually easier, especially sweet ones like her."

Zach pointed. "Here come some more fans."

Janey saw a couple of teenage girls coming toward them. "Ugh," she muttered. "Why can't people leave us alone for two seconds?"

Kitty laughed. "Don't be a grump, Janey," she said. "Everyone loves seeing dogs at the park. And we love it, too. The more people who see these dogs, the better their chances of getting adopted."

"Oh, yeah, that's true," Janey said. Suddenly she was glad that Ace wasn't with them. Otherwise he might get adopted before Mrs. Reed ever met him!

Just then Lolli poked Janey on the shoulder. "Look, there's Adam," she said.

Janey looked where her friend was pointing. Adam was coming toward them, walking a sweet-faced collie.

"I know that dog," Zach said. "Adam walks her all the time. Her owner has a really busy job."

"Like Saffron's parents?" Janey said with a giggle.

She expected Lolli to laugh. But Lolli didn't even seem to be paying attention to Janey's joke.

"That's it!" Lolli cried. "I just had the perfect fundraising idea!"

7

Lolli's Idea

"What is it?" Janey demanded. "What's your idea, Lolli?"

"Yeah, spill it," Zach added.

"Wait." Lolli led them toward Adam. "I want the whole Pet Rescue Club to hear this."

Soon Patch and Peaches were sniffing noses with the friendly collie.

"Hey, guys," Adam greeted his friends. "I just need to take this girl home and then I'll be ready for our meeting."

"Forget it," Janey said. "We're having our meeting right here and now. Lolli just had an idea."

She crossed her fingers, hoping her friend's idea was a good one. The sooner the Pet Rescue Club settled on a plan, the sooner they could help Maxi!

"Actually, you sort of gave me the idea," Lolli told Adam. Then she smiled at Kitty.

"And you did, too."

"What do you mean?" Kitty asked.

"I was thinking about what you said about how everyone likes seeing dogs in the park," Lolli explained. "And then I saw Adam and thought about how people pay him to walk their dogs. That reminded me of the walk-a-thon I did with my parents once."

"A walk-a-thon?" Adam looked interested. "I get it. You want to do a dog walk-a-thon."

"What's a walk-a-thon?" Janey asked. "And how does walking dogs raise any money?"

Lolli patted the collie. "When we did it, we were raising money for an environmental group. My parents and I asked people to sponsor us—that means they promised to pay a certain amount for every mile we walked."

"I get it." Zach nodded. "We could walk

dogs right here in the park, and ask people to sponsor us for every mile we go."

"And you could invite everyone in town to walk with their dogs to help raise more money," Kitty suggested. "People love an excuse to get out and do something with their pets."

"So you really think this will work?" Zach asked Kitty.

She smiled and nodded. "It's a fantastic idea," she said. "In fact, if your walk-a-thon is a success, maybe the shelter will do the same thing next year. We're always looking for fun ways to raise money—and raise awareness of pets in need at the same time."

"Great." Now Janey was excited. "So how do we get started?"

It turned out there was a lot to do to get ready for the walk-a-thon. On the walk back to the shelter, Kitty gave them some advice. As soon as Adam arrived after dropping off the collie, the Pet Rescue Club got to work. Janey took notes on her tablet computer while the whole group figured out what to do first.

Soon they had a plan to get started. Lolli was going to ask her parents to get permission from the town to hold the dog walk-a-thon in the park. Janey decided to start by designing a poster to hang up at local businesses. And Adam offered to send an e-mail to all the dog owners he knew asking them to take part.

"What should I do?" Zach asked.

Janey thought for a second. "We need to tell Matthew that we have a plan," she said. "Your mom knows how to reach him, right? Why don't you track him down and talk to him."

"Sure, I can do that." Zach borrowed Kitty's phone and called his mother. She was busy with a patient, but soon Russ arrived to pick him up.

"Where to, Zachie?" Russ asked.

"I need to find Matthew and Maxi," Zach said. "Do you know their phone number? Or where they live?"

"The young man with the mastiff?" the vet tech said. "Actually, I just passed them on my way here."

"You did?" Zach was surprised.

Russ nodded. "Sit tight—let's see if they're still there."

Soon he pulled to the curb beside the local high school's playing fields. Zach spotted Matthew and Maxi right away. Matthew was dressed in his running shorts and jogging in place on the school's track. Maxi was standing near him, wagging her tail.

"This will only take a second," Zach told Russ. "Can you wait for me?"

"Sure, take your time."

Zach hurried toward Matthew. Halfway there, he could hear him talking to Maxi.

"No, no, girl," the young man said. "Stay! You don't have to run with me."

"Hey, Matthew!" Zach called. "Hi!"

Both Matthew and Maxi turned. Maxi wagged her tail and hobbled toward Zach.

"It's okay, Maxi," Zach said. "I'll come to you."

He ran faster and soon reached the big dog. As he was patting her hello, Matthew came over, looking worried.

"I thought this would be a good way to spend time with Maxi," he said with a sigh.

"If I run on the track, she can hang out in the middle and watch. But she doesn't get it. She keeps trying to run with me, like always."

"She shouldn't do that," Zach said.

"I know, I know." Matthew shrugged. "I just don't know what else to do."

Once again, Zach was worried. Even if they got her the surgery she needed, would Maxi go back to running and hurt her knees again?

Zach pushed that thought aside. "Listen, I have great news," he said. "We came up with the perfect fundraiser to pay for Maxi's surgery!" He quickly told Matthew about the walk-a-thon.

"That is perfect!" the young man exclaimed. "I did a jog-a-thon once, and it was a blast. Doing it with dogs would be even more fun!"

"Yeah." Zach glanced at the big dog. "But do you think Maxi should walk that far?"

"Probably not," Matthew said with a sigh. "But maybe I can borrow a dog from a friend. I definitely want to help."

"Great." That made Zach feel better. "Tell everyone you can think of, okay? We want lots of people to join in and help us raise money."

"Will do," Matthew promised. He bent and ruffled Maxi's ears. "Did you hear that, big girl? You're going to get your surgery!"

8

Busy Busy Busy

"We need a cute name for our fundraiser." Janey clicked to save the flyer she was designing on her tablet. "Writing 'dog walk-a-thon' on every poster is too long."

Lolli nodded. The two girls were sitting at the big wooden table in Lolli's cozy, messy dining room working on the advertising for the fundraiser. Lolli's mom was on the phone in the next room talking to someone official about reserving space in the park.

"How about calling it, um…" Lolli

thought for a second. "The Doggie Dash?"

Janey wrinkled her nose. "That makes it sound like everyone has to run," she said. "I'm not sure it's clear enough, either. We want people to be excited, not confused."

Lolli nodded. "You're right. We should probably have the word 'walk' in the name."

"Walk for Cash?" Janey said. "Or the Dollar Walk?"

"But that's not clear enough either," Lolli said. "There should be something about dogs, or people might think it's a regular walk-a-thon."

"Well, we could put a dog on the poster," Janey said. But she knew her friend was right. "Okay, how about Walk Your Dog Day?"

"I guess that's okay," Lolli said uncertainly.

Janey could tell her friend didn't like her idea—she was just too nice to say so. "We don't want something okay," she said. "We want something great!" She tapped her fingers on the table. "And we need it pronto."

Just then Roscoe wandered over to see what they were doing. He rested his head on the edge of the table, staring at Janey with his big brown eyes.

"What do you think, Roscoe?" she asked, rubbing his head. "You're going to be walking in this thing—what should we call it?"

Roscoe's tongue lolled out, and he wagged his tail so hard it smacked into Lolli's leg. Lolli giggled. "Roscoe wants to call it the Walk and Slobber," she joked.

"No." Janey's eyes widened as the dog's tail smacked her again. "Roscoe's a genius! We should call it the Walk and Wag!"

Just then Lolli's mother walked into the room. "The Walk and Wag?" she said. "Is that what you're calling this thing? I like it!"

"Me, too," Lolli said. And this time Janey could tell she meant it.

"Great!" Janey patted Roscoe. "Thanks for the idea, Roscoe." Then she looked at Lolli's mom. "Did you talk to the park people?"

She smiled. "Yes, and you're on. The Walk and Wag is two weeks from Saturday."

"Two weeks?" Janey pulled her tablet closer. "Okay, let's get back to work!"

. . . .

"Great poster, kids!" Ms. Tanaka, Janey's homeroom teacher, was holding one of the

posters Janey and Lolli had printed out the day before. "I'll hang it right here where everyone can see it."

The entire Pet Rescue Club watched as the teacher hung the poster in the middle of the classroom's bulletin board. "Will you be in the Walk and Wag?" Zach asked. "You could bring Truman."

Truman was the first dog the Pet Rescue Club had helped. Ms. Tanaka had adopted him from the shelter.

"Truman and I will be there," Ms. Tanaka promised with a smile. "We love to go for walks. A walk for a good cause sounds even better!"

Lolli giggled. "Remember how you wanted a big dog at first?" she said. "Well, wait until you see Maxi. She's probably the biggest dog in town!"

"Really?" Ms. Tanaka chuckled. "I can't wait to meet her. Now take your seats—it's almost time for the bell."

As the kids hurried to their desks, Janey was still thinking about Truman. Ms. Tanaka had wanted a large dog at first. But it turned out that Truman was the perfect match for her even though he wasn't very big.

I know Mrs. Reed will be the same way, Janey thought. Everyone thinks Ace is too hyper to be a therapy dog. But I bet he'll be a perfect match, too!

. . . .

"Hi, kids," Kitty said as Janey and Lolli hurried into the shelter lobby the following Friday afternoon. "People have been asking about the Walk and Wag all week!"

"I can't believe it's only a little over a week away." Janey shivered with excitement. "Anyway, I just realized something. Lolli will be walking Roscoe. But I don't have a dog to walk. Can I walk one of the shelter dogs? Maybe Ace?"

Kitty looked thoughtful. "I think we'll have to walk him together, because he's a little too big and strong for you. Okay?"

"Okay!" said Janey. "I bet Adam and Zach will want to borrow shelter dogs, too."

....

By Sunday afternoon, it was settled. Janey, Adam, and Zach were given permission to walk shelter dogs in the fundraiser. The entire Pet Rescue Club visited the dog room to choose which dogs to take.

"What if the dog we pick gets adopted before next Saturday?" Zach wondered, tickling a friendly hound through the kennel door.

Kitty smiled. "I hope we have that problem!" she said. "And don't worry. There are always plenty of dogs here. If yours goes to a new home, you'll just have to choose a different one."

"Which dogs do you think we should pick?" Adam asked Kitty.

"I already picked mine." Janey walked over to Ace's kennel. The lively black dog jumped and barked happily when he saw her. "Ace."

"Zach's mom told Mrs. Reed about the Walk and Wag," said Janey. "And she and

Pepper are coming. She can meet Ace then."

"Okay," said Kitty. "Anything to help Ace get a good home. He's already had several adopters pass him over."

"Really?" Janey was surprised, but also glad—she didn't want anyone to adopt him except Mrs. Reed. "How come?"

"I know," Zach put in. "Because he's a spaz!"

Kitty laughed. "Well, sort of, yes," she said. "Not every dog is suitable for every type of home. You need to make sure the match is right, otherwise neither dog nor owner will be happy. Ace wouldn't do well with young children, for instance—he'd be too likely to knock them over by accident, just being himself."

"He probably wouldn't be a good dog for my family, either," Lolli said. "He might chase the goats and sheep, or run off if we didn't watch him every second."

Janey looked at Zach, expecting him to make a joke about Roscoe being too lazy to run away. But he looked thoughtful.

"I guess Matthew and Maxi aren't a very good match, either," he said. "Matthew loves to run, but Maxi is too big to run."

"Yeah." That made Janey feel sad for a moment. "I hope he figures out a way to spend time with her that doesn't hurt her knees."

"Let's get her knees fixed first," Lolli suggested. "We can worry about the rest later."

9

The Walk and Wag

"Wake up, sleepyhead. Time to get ready for the walk-a-thon!"

Janey opened her eyes. Her mother was smiling down at her.

"What time is it?" Janey asked with a yawn. Her head felt fuzzy and her eyes so heavy she could hardly keep them open.

"Six o'clock. You told me to wake you, remember? You wanted to have plenty of time to get ready for your dog walk-a-thon."

That made Janey wake up. "Oh, right,"

she exclaimed, sitting up in bed. "I can't believe it's finally here!"

Twenty minutes later, she was dressed and shoveling cereal into her mouth. Twenty minutes after that, her dad was driving her to the animal shelter.

"Are you sure you have everything you need?" he asked as he pulled to the curb. "If you forgot anything, just call me and I'll run it over to the park. And of course your mom and I will come by later to cheer you on."

"And to pay the money you promised to sponsor me, right?" Janey said.

Her dad chuckled. "Of course!"

The shelter normally didn't open until nine on Saturdays. But today Kitty was already there. So were Dr. Goldman, Zach, and Adam.

"Where's Lolli?" Janey asked.

"She's going straight to the park with Roscoe, remember?" Adam said. "We'll meet her there."

"Oh, right." There were so many details to remember that Janey had trouble keeping track of them all. She looked at Kitty. "Should we get our dogs now?"

"They're ready and waiting," Kitty responded. "I even took Ace for a quick run in the courtyard when I first got here."

"Uh-oh," Zach joked. "I hope you didn't wear him out so he can't walk very far!"

Kitty laughed. "I don't think you have to worry about that. Ace could do this walk-a-thon twice over and still have plenty of energy."

Soon they were all piling into the shelter's van with their dogs. Adam had chosen a terrier mix named Duke, and Zach was going to walk a small dog that looked like a mix of so many different breeds that the shelter had named her Misha, short for Mishmash.

Ace was so excited that he almost pulled the leash out of Janey's hand as he leaped into the van. "Hang on, boy," she said with a

laugh. "Wait for me!"

"Be careful not to let him get loose," Kitty told her. "If he does, we might never catch him."

"I'll be careful," Janey promised. She held onto the leash tightly with both hands.

When they reached the park, the work began. Lolli was waiting for them with Roscoe. Her parents were there, too, since they'd offered to help set up for the fund-raiser. Lolli's dad watched all the dogs while the others got to work.

There was a lot to do! Before long Janey was out of breath and sweating a little. But it was fun, too. They laid out a course, marking the way with colorful flags. They set up a finish line with bright tape and balloons. Lolli's parents had brought a folding table where people could sign in, and Janey taped the poster she'd made to the front and then carefully set out piles of sign-up sheets and instructions.

By the time everything was ready, people were starting to arrive. A pair of young women walking a pair of pugs hurried over. "Where do we sign up?" one of the women asked.

"Right here," Janey said. "Your dogs are super cute!"

More people were already hurrying over. Janey barely had time to give the pugs a quick pat before she had to get back to work.

....

"Wow," Lolli said. "I can't believe how many people are here!"

"And how many dogs." Janey glanced around. She and Kitty and Lolli had just started the course with Ace and Roscoe. Lolli's parents and Zach's mom had taken over at the sign-in table so the kids could participate in the walk-a-thon.

"Easy, Ace," Lolli said as the Lab mix leaped up at Roscoe. "Roscoe doesn't want to play right now."

Janey tugged on Ace's leash. The cute black dog was more excited than ever. He kept trying to dash over to say hi to every dog he saw. And that was a LOT of dogs!

But Janey kept a tight hold on his leash. Kitty walked by her side. Janey also kept a lookout for Mrs. Reed.

"Let me know if you see Mrs. Reed and Pepper," Janey said. "I want to be sure they get to meet Ace."

"Okay." Lolli glanced at Ace, who was straining against his leash and barking at a passing greyhound. "Do you think she'll like him?"

"Of course!" Janey said. "She'll love him. He's medium-sized, right?"

"True," Lolli said. "That part is a perfect

match. But like Kitty was saying…"

"Look, there they are!" Janey interrupted. "Hey, Mrs. Reed! Wait up!"

She hurried to catch up to the woman. Kitty followed them. Pepper saw them coming first and wagged his tail.

Then Ace barked and leaped toward the smaller dog. Pepper jumped back, looking alarmed.

"It's okay, baby." Mrs. Reed scooped up the Chihuahua and smiled at the girls. "Well,

hello there! I understand you kids put this whole fundraiser together to help one of Dr. Goldman's patients. What a wonderful idea!"

"Thanks," Lolli said. "Maxi's owner can't afford surgery, and we wanted to help."

"This is Ace," Janey blurted out as Ace jumped up on Mrs. Reed's legs. "He's the one in the photos we sent. He's, um, a little excited today"

"I can see that." The woman chuckled and let Ace sniff her hand. "Hello there, Ace. Aren't you a lively fellow!"

"Yes, he has lots of energy," Janey said. "That means he could be a good therapy dog, right?"

"A therapy dog? Hmm." Mrs. Reed looked at Kitty. "Maybe if he settles down a bit."

"What do you mean?" Janey said. "I thought he'd need energy to go visit lots of places with you."

"Yes, but many of the people we visit are sick or elderly or both," Mrs. Reed explained. "A dog that's too energetic can be too much for them." She patted Ace. "He's a cute fellow, though. I'm sure he could do lots of things. Maybe dog agility or something like that?"

Janey wasn't sure what to say. This wasn't turning out the way she'd planned at all! How was she going to convince Mrs. Reed that Ace really was the perfect match for her?

. . . .

"Look! There's Matthew," Adam said.

Zach saw him, too. "Hey, he brought Maxi," he said. "I hope he's not making her run. Or even walk."

"Doesn't look like it," Adam said. "They're just hanging out in the shade talking to people."

The two boys hurried over. "Hi," Zach said. "I thought you weren't going to bring Maxi."

"I couldn't stand to leave her home," Matthew said. "After all, this is all for her! Besides, we haven't been spending enough time together since she had to stop running. I don't want her to be lonely." He gave her a pat. "Anyway, my sister offered to walk with her dog in our place so we could just hang out."

"That's good," Zach said. "Look, I think Maxi likes Misha and Duke!"

The three dogs were circling one another, wagging their tails.

"Oh, Maxi gets along with everybody,"

Matthew said with a chuckle. "Even tiny dogs can boss her around and she doesn't mind a bit."

Zach nodded, remembering how calm Maxi had been with Toby the cat in the clinic waiting room. "She's pretty chill," he agreed.

"Look," Adam said. "There are Janey and Lolli."

"And Mrs. Reed," Zach added. He waved. "Guys! Over here!"

The girls and Mrs. Reed came toward them. Mrs. Reed was holding Pepper in her arms, while Ace frisked around and barked at Roscoe. Zach noticed that Janey looked kind of grumpy. But she looked that way a lot, so he didn't worry about it.

"This is Maxi," he told Mrs. Reed. "She's the one who's getting the surgery."

"Lovely to meet you, Maxi," Mrs. Reed said. As she leaned down to give the big dog a pat, Pepper wriggled in her arms, sniffing curiously at Maxi.

"You can put Pepper down," Zach said. "Maxi won't hurt him."

"Don't worry," Janey added. "I'll keep Ace away."

"Thank you, dear." Mrs. Reed set the Chihuahua on the ground. Pepper trotted over and sniffed noses with Maxi. Both dogs wagged their tails.

"Oh, and this is Matthew," Lolli added.

"I know." Mrs. Reed smiled. "Good to see you again, Matthew."

"You too, Prof," Matthew said. Glancing at the kids, he grinned. "Dr. Reed was my professor in college."

"Really?" Zach was surprised. "You're a doctor?"

"A doctor of history," Mrs. Reed said with a chuckle. "Matthew was one of my best students."

As Matthew and Mrs. Reed chatted, Zach wandered over to Janey, who had taken Ace a short distance away. Adam and Lolli came too. Kitty was sitting on a bench near them, talking to the shelter to see how things were going there.

"What's with you?" Zach asked Janey.

"Aren't you having fun?"

Janey shrugged, staring at Ace as he jumped around playfully with Duke. "I thought Mrs. Reed and Ace were a perfect match," she said. "But Pepper doesn't seem to like him much. And Mrs. Reed thinks he's too energetic to be a good therapy dog."

"Bummer," Zach said. "But don't worry, there are lots of other medium-sized dogs at the shelter. Maybe she'll like one of them better."

He glanced over at Adam to see what he thought. But Adam was staring back toward Mrs. Reed and Matthew. "Do you see that?" he said.

"See what?" Zach looked where Adam was looking. Pepper was sitting between Maxi's front legs. Maxi was peering down

at the little dog, staying very still. Her tail
thumped against the ground as she wagged
it. Mrs. Reed's hand was resting on the big
dog's head, her fingers idly scratching at
Maxi's ears as she talked to Matthew.

Zach looked at Adam, who was smiling.
"I just had an idea," Adam whispered to him.
"Let's go find your mom!"

10

Happily Ever After

By the time she finished the course, Janey was feeling happier. "Are you okay?" Lolli asked. "Even though Ace and Pepper didn't get along?"

"I'm fine," Janey said. "Anyway, it's not hopeless, right? Maybe we should try again on a less busy day. The two of them might get along better then."

Lolli looked uncertain. "Maybe," she said. "But I'm still not sure Mrs. Reed will—"

"Hey!" Adam interrupted breathlessly, jogging up to them with Duke at his heel.

Zach and Misha were right behind them. "We need to talk to you about something."

"What?" Janey asked.

Adam glanced over his shoulder. "Did you notice how well Maxi gets along with little Pepper?"

Janey frowned. Was he trying to rub it in? "Yeah, we know," she grumbled. "Maxi gets along with everyone."

"Exactly." Zach grinned. "And we just checked with my mom—she says mastiffs often make good therapy dogs."

"So what?" Janey said. "Matthew doesn't have enough time to spend with Maxi as it is. How's he supposed to turn her into a therapy dog, too?"

"He's not," Zach said. "Mrs. Reed can do that!"

"Huh?" Lolli blinked.

"It was Adam's idea," Zach said. "He was thinking about how Matthew and Maxi are mismatched."

Adam nodded. "It's like Kitty was saying that time. Some dogs need certain kinds of homes."

"And Matthew's home is the wrong one for Maxi," Zach went on. "He loves to run, and he doesn't have much spare time."

"But running is bad for Maxi." Janey was starting to get it. "So what are you saying? That he should take Maxi to the shelter?"

"No way! He'd never do that," Zach said. "But he might give her to a home that's a better match—especially if he already knows her new owner."

Lolli gasped. "Mrs. Reed!"

"But she wants a medium-sized dog," Janey said. "Maxi is definitely not medium-sized."

Zach shrugged. "She wants a dog that's sturdy enough to visit kids. Maxi definitely is that. And she seemed to like her."

"But what about Ace?" Janey glanced at the black dog, who was trying to convince Misha to play with him.

The two boys traded a grin. "She's a little slow today, isn't she?" Zach commented.

Adam laughed. "Don't you get it?" he told Janey. "We found Ace's perfect match, too—Matthew! He needs a dog that can keep up with lots of running."

Now it was Janey's turn to gasp. "And that's Ace!" She tugged on the leash. "Come on, let's go tell them!"

. . . .

"It's amazing how things worked out, isn't it?" Janey asked Mrs. Reed.

It was a little over a week later and the two of them were in the waiting room of the Critter Clinic, along with the rest of the Pet Rescue Club. Matthew was there, too. So was Ace. The cute black dog was lying on the floor under his new owner's chair, taking a nap.

Janey smiled when she saw that. "I never thought I'd see Ace being so still," she said.

Matthew chuckled. "We went on a nice long run this morning," he said. "He's all tuckered out."

"As they say, a tired dog is a good dog." Mrs. Reed chuckled and patted Pepper, who was sitting on her lap. Then she glanced toward the door leading to the back room, looking anxious. "I wonder how Maxi is doing."

"Don't worry," Lolli told her. "Zach's mom is the best. She'll fix her."

Janey nodded. But she also crossed her fingers. She hoped Maxi's surgery went well so she could begin her new career as a therapy dog.

At first, both Mrs. Reed and Matthew weren't sure about Adam's plan. But the more they discussed it, the more they realized how perfect it was. Maxi would get a good home where Matthew could visit her. He was sad at the thought of giving her up, but happy at the idea that she'd have a job she was good at—being a therapy dog—and would be getting lots more attention, too.

Mrs. Reed hadn't planned on getting such a large dog. But then she decided that size didn't matter. The important thing was Maxi's personality, and that was perfect for therapy work. She was even going to pay for Maxi's surgery herself, so the money from the Walk and Wag could go to the shelter!

As for Matthew, one test run was all it had taken to convince him that Ace would be able to keep up with him.

"It's the perfect happily ever after," Janey murmured as she thought about how well everything had worked out.

Adam heard her and looked over. "Don't jinx it," he said. "It's not happy ever after until Maxi is safely out of surgery."

Janey nodded and stared at the door leading to the clinic's back room. All of them were waiting for the surgery to be over. "Why's it taking so long?" she wondered.

"You don't want Mom to rush it," Zach reminded her.

"I know," Janey said. "But—"

She cut herself off as the door opened and Dr. Goldman stepped out. She was smiling as she peeled off her surgical gloves.

"I won't keep you in suspense," she said. "The surgery went very well. Maxi should recover fully."

"Hooray!" Janey cried, leaping to her feet and doing a happy dance.

That woke up Ace. He leaped to his feet, barking and wagging his tail and doing his own happy dance. Pepper barked, too.

"You said it," Janey told both dogs with a giggle. "Now it really is another happily ever after for the Pet Rescue Club!"

THE END

The Right Dog for the Right Home

There are lots of dog breeds out there—and countless adorable mixed breed dogs as well. It can be tempting to choose the cutest dog, or the friendliest, or one that reminds you of a dog from TV or the movies. But it's important to make sure the dog you adopt fits your personality and lifestyle. Do you spend a lot of time outdoors, or prefer quieter pastimes? Do you live in the country or the city? Do you like to keep your house spotless, or will a little—or a lot—of dog hair not bother you? Are you confident enough to handle a dominant breed, or do you prefer someone sweet and easygoing?

All of these questions and more are important to consider. Talk to your local shelter workers about finding the right match, or check out the many resources online to help narrow it down.

ASPCA's "Meet Your Match" program

(http://www.aspca.org/adopt/meet-your-match)

Good luck finding your perfect pooch—and your happily ever after!

Meet the Real Maxi!

Maxi, the mastiff who was too big to run, was inspired by a real-life animal rescue story. A mastiff named Millie was given to a mastiff rescue group when she was only two years old. Her knees were injured, just like Maxi's, but a caring new owner adopted her and got her the surgery and care she needed to become healthy again. After that, Millie became a certified therapy dog—just like Maxi!

Look for these other books in the
PET RESCUE CLUB
series!

1 A New Home for Truman

Janey can't have a pet of her own because of her father's allergies. Her love for animals is so strong, though, that it leads her and her friends to create the Pet Rescue Club to help animals in need, like Truman the dog!

2 No Time for Hallie

Can the Pet Rescue Club help a senior cat find a new home when her owners decide they no longer have the time or attention to give her?

3 The Lonely Pony

When Adam finds Lola, a neglected pony, the Pet Rescue Club is determined to find her a better home, despite the challenges of caring properly for a small horse.